Edited by Deborah Campbell-Todd
Cover design by Oxprint Ltd

ISBN 0 86112 746 3
Published by Brimax Books Ltd, Newmarket, England 1991.
Printed in Hong Kong

FOLLOW MY LEADER

by Lucy Kincaid
Illustrated by Eric Kincaid

Brimax Books · Newmarket · England

Follow the Leader

"I wish they would go and play somewhere else," sighed Will. Pa and Will were working in Mrs Johnson's kitchen. They were having a difficult time. Mrs Johnson had so many children even she didn't know exactly how many she had. She counted them sometimes when they were in bed, but the answer never came out the same. The only time the house was quiet was when they were all tucked up in bed and ASLEEP. The rest of the time their little voices never stopped talking, and their little fingers were into everything.

6

"Who has taken my screwdriver?" asked Pa. He had put it down to look for a screw he had dropped and now it was gone.

"Not me! Not me!" shouted everyone, except the one who had it. And he was lost in the crowd.

"We will never get this job finished," sighed Pa, as Rooney rescued his screwdriver and handed it back to him.

"Can't you take them somewhere and play with them?" Will asked Rooney.

Rooney looked round at the climbing, giggling, crawling, jumping, poking, pulling, pushing, yelling, shouting, fighting, laughing crowd of children and said, "What? All of them?"

Someone else had heard Will and thought the idea a good one.

"Follow the leader . . . follow the leader . . . ,"
shouted the rabbit with the loudest voice.

"Must I?" asked Rooney with a pleading look at
Pa.

"Please . . . ," said Pa, with an equally pleading
look at Rooney. "Please Rooney, for all our sakes."

"Rooney's the leader . . . follow the leader . . . ,"
shouted the rabbit with the loudest voice.

"Hooray!" shouted all the other voices that only
a second before had been shouting a hundred other
things.

Before Rooney had time to gather his wits and
escape he was being chased by a squealing, waving,
jumping, skipping, running, scrambling, leaping,
shouting, horde of children.

8

"Looks more like chase the leader to me," said Will. "Poor Rooney."

"We'll get the job done quickly with them out of the way," said Pa. "And the sooner we get it done the sooner we can rescue Rooney."

Aunt Tilda was in her garden sweeping up leaves when Rooney rushed past with his followers.

"Can't stop!" panted Rooney.

Aunt Tilda didn't know they were playing a game. She thought Rooney needed rescuing. Which he did in a way.

She ran into the middle of the mob waving her broom and shouting, "Stop . . . stop . . ."

Not one of them reached higher than her apron strings. Not one of them heard her shouting stop. They were shouting too loudly themselves.

9

"It's follow the leader . . . come and play . . ."
Someone caught hold of her skirt, someone caught
hold of her broom. They pulled her along with them.
But not for long. Noisy, excited children did not
frighten Aunt Tilda.

With no children getting in the way Pa and Will
soon had the job finished. They started to pack up
their tools.

"Have you noticed how quiet it is," said Will
suddenly. "I hope Rooney is alright. I hope those
children haven't chased him into the river, or locked
him in a barn somewhere."

"Of course he is alright," said Pa. "Rooney can
look after himself."

But when it stayed quiet and there was no sound or
sight of Rooney and children at all, not even in the
distance, Pa began to get worried himself.

10

Mrs Johnson was puzzled too. "Too much quiet isn't a good thing," she said.

They decided to investigate.

Everywhere was deserted. There were no children playing. There were no birds twittering in the hedges. There were no dogs barking in the distance. It started to seem as though there really was something to be worried about.

"Do you think the Pied Piper has passed through the village?" said Will.

"Shush," said Pa, "Don't say such things, you will worry Mrs Johnson."

They were standing in a huddle in the middle of the road trying to decide what to do when they suddenly caught the sound of Aunt Tilda's voice droning on the wind.

At least she hadn't been magicked away. "She may have seen something," said Pa. "Let's go and ask her."

11

"Aunt Tilda seems to have a lot to say," said Pa as they turned in at the garden gate. Her voice was droning on and on like bees in summer weather.

"She can't be talking to herself, she must have a visitor," said Will.

Aunt Tilda's voice was coming from the orchard at the back of the house.

"I don't believe my eyes," gasped Pa, as they turned the corner. Mrs Johnson just stared.

Aunt Tilda was sitting on a stool in the middle of the orchard with Rooney at her side, and all around her on the grass were the Johnson children. They were sitting with hands and feet still, and with voices silent. Aunt Tilda was telling them a story about castles and giants and magic and for the first time in their lives they were all quiet at the same time.

12

Rooney saw their surprised faces and put his finger to his lips.

"I didn't know Aunt Tilda could tell stories like that," said Will when the story was finished.

"More . . . more," shouted the children jumping to their feet and becoming an unruly mob.

"If you walk home quietly, and in an orderly fashion," said Aunt Tilda firmly, "I will tell you another story tomorrow."

To everyone's surprise, especially Mrs Johnson's, the children did as they were told.

"Will you teach me how to tell stories" said Mrs Johnson.

"I shall be glad to," said Aunt Tilda. "Children like to sit quietly sometimes."

"Isn't Aunt Tilda wonderful," sighed Rooney.

13

Tall Tales

"Is anyone at home?" asked a voice at the woodshed door.

"Come in," said Pa. "What can we do for you?"

"I want a new lock put on my sea-chest. The salt air has got into this one and made it sticky. I can't turn the key in it," said the stranger. He took a key from his pocket and showed them what he meant.

"I'll see what I can do," said Pa.

"Whatever you do, can you do it while I wait," said the sailor. "I carry everything I own in that chest and I'm off to sea tomorrow."

Pa said he would try. He knew he had a suitable lock somewhere. He found it, at last, in a box under the bench.

Rooney had never met a sailor before.

"Have you sailed all round the world?" he asked.

"A hundred times," said the sailor.

"You must have had many adventures," said Rooney.

"Thousands," said the sailor.

"You must have lots of stories to tell," said Will.

"Millions," said the sailor. "I'll tell you a few while I wait." He needed no persuading. Like all sailors he enjoyed telling stories about his adventures.

Before he began, he took off his seaboots and made himself comfortable. This was going to take a long time.

He told them stories of the South Seas and the Arctic, of being shipwrecked and becalmed, of coral islands and cannibals, of pirates and mermaids.

The stories, and the sailor's voice, went on and on and on and on. Rooney was listening as hard as Pa and Will but his ears got tired. He looked around for something to do while he gave his ears a rest.

The sailor's boots were right beside him. Rooney had never seen boots like them before. They were long and black. Very long and very black. Rooney peeped inside one. It looked like a long dark tunnel. It smelt of rubber, and the sea. It was like a magnet to Rooney's nose. He crept into it, further . . . and further . . . until he disappeared altogether and only the tip of his tail was showing.

When he reached the toe he tried to turn round so that he could come out. The boot fitted him like a sock. He couldn't turn. Neither could he wriggle out backwards. He was stuck.

16

The sailor was telling an exciting story about a giant sea-slug that swallowed ships when he suddenly stopped, right in the middle of a sentence.

"Go on," said Will eagerly. He wanted to hear how the sailor had escaped with his life.

"Is something wrong?" asked Pa as he saw the expression on the sailor's face change.

In answer, the sailor pointed to the floor behind them.

Something in his expression made both Pa and Will turn quickly and look for themselves. What they saw made them gasp, and without a moment's hesitation all three of them scrambled up onto the bench.

A large black slug, was wriggling and squirming its way across the floor. At least . . . they thought it was

17

a large black slug.

"Don't let it get up here," shouted Will, trying to make himself invisible and not managing to do it at all.

"Where's Rooney?" shouted Pa in alarm, noticing for the first time that Rooney was not there with them.

"That thing's eaten him . . . look . . . I can see Rooney's tail . . . it's eaten Rooney . . . what are we going to do?" Will was jumping about on top of the bench like an indian doing a war dance. He had forgotten about making himself invisible.

"Do something!" he said to the sailor. But the sailor had only met sea-slugs in stories. He didn't know what to do with them in real life.

18

Rooney could tell something was happening. But he couldn't tell what. He struggled to get out of the boot so that he could find out.

"Jump on it," said the sailor. "You're bigger than me," he said to Will. "Jump on it . . . squash it . . ."

It was fortunate for Rooney that Pa had got over his fright. Pa recognised Rooney's tail. He guessed what had happened. Will bent his knees and got ready to jump. Pa caught hold of him round the waist and stopped him just in time.

"Let me go . . . ," shouted Will. "It's got Rooney. I've got to rescue Rooney."

"It is Rooney, you fool," said Pa, holding on with all his might. He was the one saving Rooney, not Will.

Will didn't look as though he believed Pa. He still wanted to jump.

"He's crawled inside the sailor's boot," explained Pa.

"Then why doesn't he come out?" said Will, shaking like a leaf at the thought of what he might have done to Rooney.

"He must be stuck," said Pa getting down from the bench to investigate.

"Are you alright in there?" he asked speaking to the toe of the boot.

"I see," he said when he heard what the boot had to say in reply.

"I was right," said Pa. "He's stuck."

While Will sat on the floor and held the toe of the boot between his knees, Pa pulled as gently as he could on Rooney's tail. Between them they managed to pull Rooney free.

"What was all that commotion about?" asked Rooney. "Did I miss something? Has something happened? And what is he doing on the bench?"

The sailor was watching and remembering so he could put everything that had happened into another story.

"You wouldn't believe us if we told you," said Pa.

"The best stories happen in real life," said the sailor as he left with his sea-chest. "Always remember that."

"What DID he mean?" asked Rooney. Will told him, and Pa was absolutely right, Rooney didn't believe a word of it.

"Now you are making up stories about things that don't really happen," said Rooney. "Mistaking a boot for a giant sea-slug . . . that's silly. No one would believe that."

And nothing they said could persuade him otherwise so they gave up trying.

21

Sawdust

Will had been sawing all the morning and there was a lot of sawdust under the bench.

It was still lying there when Aunt Tilda paid the woodshed a visit later in the day. Rooney saw her looking at it out of the corner of her eye and rushed for the broom.

"I meant to sweep it up this morning," he said, "But I . . . ." ·

"Forgot," said Aunt Tilda, finishing the sentence for him. Instead of tutting at him, as he expected, Aunt Tilda looked thoughtful.

As Rooney scooped the piled up sawdust into a box, she said, "Are you going to use that?"

"Er . . . no . . . ," said Rooney.

"Can I have it?" asked Aunt Tilda.

"I suppose so," said Rooney.

Aunt Tilda took the box from him and on the way out of the woodshed passed Will coming in.

"What are you going to do with all that sawdust, Aunt Tilda?" asked Will.

"Do I ask you what you are doing with a box of sawdust when you have one?" she asked.

"Well, no," said Will.

"Then don't expect an answer when you ask me," she said.

"She's up to something," said Will as he watched her marching away.

"She's up to something," he said again the next day, when she came to the woodshed and collected another boxful of sawdust. She still wouldn't tell them what she wanted it for. The mystery was deepening.

The next day they were waiting for her. They had the sawdust ready in a box.

As she marched away with it two shadowy figures slipped out of the woodshed and followed her. They had flat brown caps pulled down over their foreheads, and scarves wrapped round their faces.

Every time Aunt Tilda looked over her shoulder they hid behind a bush, or a wall. Once they fell flat on their faces in the grass and pretended to be part of the ground.

She didn't go home. She went to a house in the village. She was expected because the door opened as she walked up the path and she went inside.

"What do we do now?" asked Rooney, his voice muffled by his scarf.

"Look inside of course," said Will.

They sneaked into the garden and up to the
window. Aunt Tilda and three of her friends were
sitting round the table wrapping things in pieces of
tissue paper. There were heaps of unwrapped
things and heaps of wrapped things but no sign of the
box of sawdust.

Rooney squashed his nose closer to the window to
get a better view. It made a tiny squeak. Will
squashed his nose against the window to get a better
view. His nose was bigger and made a bigger squeak.
Aunt Tilda heard it and looked up.

"It's a good thing we are in disguise," said Will as
they quickly ducked below the level of the windowsill.

"Do you think she saw us?" asked Rooney.

"I don't think so," whispered Will. "I think we are safe."

Will was wrong. Aunt Tilda HAD seen them. She knew exactly who they were. The disguise didn't fool her.

She threw open the window and hit them both over the head with a rolled up newspaper.

"That!" she said, as she bopped Will, "is for peeping, Master Will."

"That!" she said, as she bopped Rooney, "is for peeping, Master Rooney."

And then she slammed the window shut and caught the peaks of both their caps in it.

"Oh!" said Will.

"I'm going home," said Rooney wriggling out of his cap, and he went, leaving Will to rescue the caps on his own.

The next time Aunt Tilda came into the woodshed she said nothing about what had happened and neither did they. Though she must have said something to Pa because he looked at them and laughed.

"I've got a job for you two," he said.

"Good," whispered Will, "we can escape from Aunt Tilda's steely gaze."

Will was wrong again. Aunt Tilda wanted two barrels for some mysterious purpose of her own, and Will and Rooney had to roll them all the way home for her. Aunt Tilda's steely gaze followed them every step of the way.

"There's something going on," said Will as they walked home. "I wish I knew what it was."

"I wish you would stop saying that," said Rooney. "It only gets us into trouble."

The next time they saw the barrels was at the harvest supper. Harvest supper was always held in Farmer John's barn. There was plenty of room and it didn't matter if it rained.

"Those are Aunt Tilda's barrels," said Will, nudging Rooney.

"I wonder what they are doing here?"

"I'm not going anywhere near them," said Rooney. He meant what he said when he said it.

After supper it was time to play games. Presently little parcels began to appear . . . .

"Where are they coming from?" asked Will.

"From the brantubs of course," said Pa, pointing to the barrels. "Didn't you know? Didn't Aunt Tilda tell you?"

They rushed to look. The barrels were full of sawdust, and buried in the sawdust were the little parcels wrapped in paper. The mystery was explained.

But before Rooney and Will had a chance to dip into the brantubs themselves Aunt Tilda arrived at their elbows.

"Why didn't you tell us what you were doing with

the sawdust?" asked Will.

"Would have done if you hadn't peeped," she said. "You peeped so you didn't deserve to share the secret."

She made them wait until the very last before she let them have their dip into the brantub.

"I hope there will be something left for us," said Rooney.

Aunt Tilda said they would have to wait and find out, but she knew there would be because she had counted the parcels herself.